CYNTHIA RYLANT

POPPLETON
Forever

BOOK FOUR

Illustrated by
MARK TEAGUE

THE BLUE SKY PRESS
An Imprint of Scholastic Inc. · New York

To Mark and Emily
M. T.

THE BLUE SKY PRESS

Text copyright © 1998 by Cynthia Rylant
Illustrations copyright © 1998 by Mark Teague
All rights reserved.

For information regarding permission, please write to:
Permissions Department,
The Blue Sky Press, an imprint of Scholastic Inc.,
555 Broadway, New York, New York 10012.
The Blue Sky Press is a registered trademark of Scholastic Inc.
Library of Congress catalog card number: 97-14047
ISBN 0-590-84843-7
10 9 8 7 6 5 4 3 2 1   8 9 0/0 01 02 03
Printed in Mexico   49
First printing, August 1998
Designed by Kathleen Westray

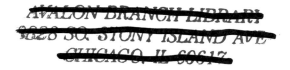
CONTENTS

THE TREE

Poppleton planted a new little tree
in his yard.

It was a dogwood.

Poppleton liked it very much.

He watered it every day.

He gave it tree food.

He staked it against the wind.

The little tree grew strong and fast.

Poppleton was pleased.

Then one day the tree looked awful.

Its leaves drooped.

Its bark peeled.

It turned from green to brown.

"Oh no!" said Poppleton,

when he saw his tree.

He called the tree doctor.

"Come right away!" said Poppleton.

The tree doctor came

to look at Poppleton's tree.

He tapped it.

He stroked it.

He felt its trunk and leaves.

The tree doctor said to Poppleton,

"This tree needs something,

but I don't know what it is."

"Can't you just give it a pill?"
asked Poppleton.
"It isn't sick," said the tree doctor.
"It *needs* something."
Poppleton did not know
what his little tree needed.

He tapped it.

He stroked it.

He felt its trunk and leaves.

But he did not know.

Poppleton sat up with his tree all night,
wondering what it needed.

"What does my tree need?" Poppleton
asked Newhouse, the delivery dog.
"A bone?" said Newhouse.

Poppleton bought a bird feeder
for his little tree.

Poppleton gave the tree a bone,
but it didn't help.

Poppleton went to see Cherry Sue.
"What does my tree need?"
Poppleton asked Cherry Sue.
Cherry Sue looked out her window
at the little tree.
She thought and thought.

Then she said, "If I were that tree,
I would need a bird feeder."
"A bird feeder?" asked Poppleton.
"Trees want birds," said Cherry Sue.
"Why do you think they hold out
their arms all day?"

A sparrow came,
and a leaf turned green.

A cardinal came,
and another leaf turned green.

A bluebird came,
and three leaves turned green.

19

Poppleton's tree got better.

Soon all of its leaves were green.

"You are a pretty smart llama,"
Poppleton told Cherry Sue.
"You are a pretty nice pig,"
Cherry Sue told him.
Then they had lemonade
and watched the birds.

THE COLD

Poppleton had an awful cold.

He sneezed and sneezed.

Tissues were all over his house.

His neighbor Cherry Sue
knocked on his door.
She had a bowl full of ten oranges.
"Oranges are good for colds,
Poppleton," said Cherry Sue.

Poppleton gave the tree a bone,
but it didn't help.

Poppleton went to see Cherry Sue.
"What does my tree need?"
Poppleton asked Cherry Sue.
Cherry Sue looked out her window
at the little tree.
She thought and thought.

Then she said, "If I were that tree,
I would need a bird feeder."
"A bird feeder?" asked Poppleton.
"Trees want birds," said Cherry Sue.
"Why do you think they hold out
their arms all day?"

Poppleton bought a bird feeder
for his little tree.

A sparrow came,
and a leaf turned green.

A cardinal came,
and another leaf turned green.

A bluebird came,
and three leaves turned green.

Poppleton's tree got better.

Soon all of its leaves were green.

"You are a pretty smart llama,"
Poppleton told Cherry Sue.
"You are a pretty nice pig,"
Cherry Sue told him.
Then they had lemonade
and watched the birds.

THE COLD

Poppleton had an awful cold.

He sneezed and sneezed.

Tissues were all over his house.

His neighbor Cherry Sue

knocked on his door.

She had a bowl full of ten oranges.

"Oranges are good for colds,

Poppleton," said Cherry Sue.

Poppleton nodded his head.

He was too stuffy to talk.

Cherry Sue went home, and

Poppleton peeled an orange.

AH-CHOOOOOO!

The orange flew out of Poppleton's
hands and landed in the fish tank.
Poppleton peeled another orange.

AH-CHOOOOOO!

The orange flew out of Poppleton's
hands and landed in the piano.
Poppleton peeled a third orange.

Later Cherry Sue knocked
on Poppleton's door.
She had a bowl full of eggs.
"Eggs are good for colds, Poppleton,"
said Cherry Sue.
"Uh-oh," said Poppleton.

WALLPAPER

Poppleton bought some wallpaper
for his kitchen.
He asked his friend Hudson
to help him hang it.

33

"Sure," said Hudson.

Hudson came over

on Saturday morning.

Poppleton and Hudson put some glue
on the back of the wallpaper.
Then they tried to hang it on the wall.
"Hold up your side, Hudson,"
said Poppleton.

Fillmore came over to help.

"Hold up your part, Fillmore,"
said Poppleton.

Poppleton looked over at Fillmore.

Fillmore was chewing on the paper.

Hmmm, thought Poppleton.
Maybe I shouldn't have asked a goat
to help hang wallpaper.
"I'll call Cherry Sue to help us,"
said Poppleton.

Cherry Sue came over to help.
"Hold up your part, Cherry Sue,"
said Poppleton.
Poppleton looked over at Cherry Sue.
Cherry Sue was stuck to the glue.

Hmmm, thought Poppleton.
*Maybe I shouldn't have asked a llama
to help hang wallpaper.*

"How can I hang wallpaper," Poppleton complained to them all, "when Hudson is a mouse, and Fillmore is a goat, and Cherry Sue is a llama!"

The three friends looked at Poppleton.

"Oh dear," said Poppleton, ashamed.

"I can stand on a ladder," said Hudson.

"I can eat a big breakfast first,"
said Fillmore.

"I can get a haircut," said Cherry Sue.

44

Poppleton looked at his three dear friends.

Such good friends.

"And I can take you all out for ice cream!"
said Poppleton.

Which he did.

On their way back home, Poppleton traded the wallpaper for some paint.

His friends were the finest painters
in town.

48